THIS BOOK

BELONGS TO:

....

....

Appley Dapply's Nursery Rhymes

APPLEY DAPPLY'S NURSERY RHYMES

BY

BEATRIX POTTER

A PETER RABBIT™

110th Anniversary Edition

FREDERICK WARNE

FREDERICK WARNE

Published by the Penguin Group
Penguin Books Ltd., 80 Strand, London WC2R 0RL, England
Penguin Group (USA) Inc., 375 Hudson Street, New York, New York 10014, USA
Penguin Group (Australia), 250 Camberwell Road, Camberwell,
Victoria 3124, Australia (a division of Pearson Australia Group Pty. Ltd.)
Penguin Group (Canada), 90 Eglinton Avenue East, Suite 700, Toronto,
Ontario M4P 2Y3, Canada (a division of Pearson Penguin Canada Inc.)
Penguin Books India Pvt. Ltd., 11 Community Centre, Panchsheel Park, New Delhi—110 017,
Penguin Group (NZ), 67 Apollo Drive, Rosedale, Auckland 0632,
New Zealand (a division of Pearson New Zealand Ltd.)
Penguin Books (South Africa) (Pty.) Ltd, 24 Sturdee Avenue, Rosebank, Johannesburg 2196, South A

Penguin Books Ltd., Registered Offices: 80 Strand, London WC2R 0RL, England

Website: www.peterrabbit.com

First published by Frederick Warne in 1917
First published with reset text and new reproductions
of Beatrix Potter's illustrations in 2002
This edition published in 2011

003 - 10 9 8 7 6 5 4 3

Colour reproduction by
EAE Creative Colour Ltd, Norwich
Printed and bound in China

PUBLISHER'S NOTE

Appley Dapply's Nursery Rhymes had a long history even prior to its publication. Beatrix began painting images of the old woman who lived in a shoe as early as 1893, and the idea of a book of rhymes was discussed with Beatrix's fiancé and original editor Norman Warne but not pursued.

The project was revived in 1917, when Frederick Warne & Co. requested a new story but Beatrix was occupied with her farm and suggested Appley Dapply as an alternative. 'The old drawings are some of them better than any I could do now,' wrote Beatrix to editor Fruing Warne, lamenting the decline in her eyesight. As a result, the little volume is a fascinating mixture of illustration styles from the early and middle stages of her career.

APPLEY DAPPLY,
a little brown mouse,
Goes to the cupboard
in somebody's house.

In somebody's cupboard
there's everything nice,
Cake, cheese, jam, biscuits,
—all charming for mice!

APPLEY DAPPLY
has little sharp eyes,
And Appley Dapply
is *so* fond of pies!

Now who is this knocking
at Cotton-tail's door?
Tap tappit! Tap tappit!
She's heard it before?

AND when she peeps out
there is nobody there,
But a present of carrots
put down on the stair.

HARK! I hear it again!
Tap, tap, tappit! Tap tappit!
Why—I really believe
it's a little black rabbit!

OLD MR. PRICKLEPIN
has never a cushion
to stick his pins in,
His nose is black
and his beard is gray,
And he lives in an ash stump
over the way.

YOU know the old woman
who lived in a shoe?
And had so many children
she didn't know what to do?

H.B.P.

I THINK if she lived
in a little shoe-house—
That little old woman
was surely a mouse!

DIGGORY DIGGORY DELVET!
A little old man in black velvet
He digs and he delves –
You can see for yourselves
The mounds dug by Diggory Delvet

GRAVY and potatoes
In a good brown pot –
Put them in the oven,
And serve them very hot!

THERE once was an amiable
guinea-pig,
Who brushed back his hair
like a periwig—

He wore a sweet tie,
As blue as the sky –

H. B. P.

AND his whiskers and buttons were very big.

THE END

THIS BOOK

BELONGS TO:

Klara

THE TALE OF *Tom Kitten*

THE TALE OF
TOM KITTEN

BY

BEATRIX POTTER

A PETER RABBIT™

110th Anniversary Edition

FREDERICK WARNE

DEDICATED TO ALL

PICKLES

— ESPECIALLY TO THOSE THAT GET

UPON MY GARDEN WALL

FREDERICK WARNE

Published by the Penguin Group
Penguin Books Ltd., 80 Strand, London WC2R 0RL, England
Penguin Group (USA) Inc., 375 Hudson Street, New York, New York 10014, USA
Penguin Group (Australia), 250 Camberwell Road, Camberwell,
Victoria 3124, Australia (a division of Pearson Australia Group Pty. Ltd.)
Penguin Group (Canada), 90 Eglinton Avenue East, Suite 700, Toronto,
Ontario M4P 2Y3, Canada (a division of Pearson Penguin Canada Inc.)
Penguin Books India Pvt. Ltd., 11 Community Centre, Panchsheel Park, New Delhi—110 017, I
Penguin Group (NZ), 67 Apollo Drive, Rosedale, Auckland 0632,
New Zealand (a division of Pearson New Zealand Ltd.)
Penguin Books (South Africa) (Pty.) Ltd, 24 Sturdee Avenue, Rosebank, Johannesburg 2196, South A

Penguin Books Ltd., Registered Offices: 80 Strand, London WC2R 0RL, England

Website: www.peterrabbit.com

First published by Frederick Warne in 1907
First published with reset text and new reproductions
of Beatrix Potter's illustrations in 2002
This edition published in 2011

003 - 10 9 8 7 6 5 4 3

Colour reproduction by
EAE Creative Colour Ltd, Norwich
Printed and bound in China

PUBLISHER'S NOTE

At the time Beatrix Potter was working on *The Tale of Tom Kitten*, she had recently purchased the Lake District farm Hill Top. The house, its garden and the village cats all feature in the illustrations. Beatrix's publisher Harold Warne, whose daughter Louie had a mischievous pet kitten, was confident that Tom would make an appealing hero. He was proved right, and in 1914 Harold Warne even had a request for a musical version of the story, though Beatrix, with characteristic directness, dismissed the proposal for Tom Kitten in verse as 'considerable twaddle'.

Tom Kitten has continued to appeal to popular imagination and the many fans who visit Hill Top Farm today enjoy seeing 'Tom Kitten's house', as Beatrix called it, preserved exactly as it appears in her illustrations.

ONCE UPON A TIME there were three little kittens, and their names were—

Mittens,

Tom Kitten,

and Moppet.

They had dear little fur coats of their own; and they tumbled about the doorstep and played in the dust.

BUT one day their mother – Mrs. Tabitha Twitchit – expected friends to tea; so she fetched the kittens indoors, to wash and dress them, before the fine company arrived.

First she scrubbed their faces (this one is Moppet).

THEN she brushed their fur
(this one is Mittens).

THEN she combed their tails and whiskers (this is Tom Kitten).

Tom was very naughty, and he scratched.

MRS. TABITHA dressed Moppet and Mittens in clean pinafores and tuckers; and then she took all sorts of elegant uncomfortable clothes out of a chest of drawers, in order to dress up her son Thomas.

TOM KITTEN was very fat, and he had grown; several buttons burst off. His mother sewed them on again.

When the three kittens were ready, Mrs. Tabitha unwisely turned them out into the garden, to be out of the way while she made hot buttered toast.

"Now keep your frocks clean, children! You must walk on your hind legs. Keep away from the dirty ash-pit, and from Sally Henny-penny, and from the pig-stye and the Puddle-ducks."

MOPPET and Mittens walked down the garden path unsteadily. Presently they trod upon their pinafores and fell on their noses.

When they stood up there were several green smears!

"LET us climb up the rockery, and sit on the garden wall," said Moppet.

They turned their pinafores back to front, and went up with a skip and a jump; Moppet's white tucker fell down into the road.

Tom Kitten was quite unable to jump when walking upon his hind legs in trousers. He came up the rockery by degrees, breaking the ferns, and shedding buttons right and left.

He was all in pieces when he reache
the top of the wall.

Moppet and Mittens tried to pu
him together; his hat fell off, and th
rest of his buttons burst.

WHILE they were in difficulties, there was a pit pat paddle pat! and the three Puddle-ducks came along the hard high road, marching one behind the other and doing the goose step — pit pat paddle pat! pit pat waddle pat!

THEY stopped and stood in a row, and stared up at the kittens. They had very small eyes and looked surprised.

THEN the two duck-birds, Rebeccah and Jemima Puddle-duck, picked up the hat and tucker and put them on.

Mittens laughed so that she fel off the wall. Moppet and Tom descended after her; the pinafores and all the rest of Tom's clothes came off on the way down.

"Come! Mr. Drake Puddle-duck," said Moppet — "Come and help us to dress him! Come and button up Tom!"

Mr. Drake Puddle-duck advanced in a slow sideways manner, and picked up the various articles.

BUT he put them on *himself!* They fitted him even worse than Tom Kitten.

"It's a very fine morning!" said Mr. Drake Puddle-duck.

AND he and Jemima and Rebeccah Puddle-duck set off up the road, keeping step – pit pat, paddle pat! pit pat, waddle pat!

THEN Tabitha Twitchit came down the garden and found her kittens on the wall with no clothes on.

SHE pulled them off the wall, smacked them, and took them back to the house.

"My friends will arrive in a minute, and you are not fit to be seen; I am affronted," said Mrs. Tabitha Twitchit.

SHE sent them upstairs; and I am sorry to say she told her friends that they were in bed with the measles; which was not true.

QUITE the contrary; they were not in bed; *not* in the least.

Somehow there were very extra-ordinary noises over-head, which disturbed the dignity and repose of the tea-party.

AND I think that some day I shall have to make another, larger, book, to tell you more about Tom Kitten!

As for the Puddle-ducks – they went into a pond.

The clothes all came off directly, because there were no buttons.

AND Mr. Drake Puddle-duck, and Jemima and Rebeccah, have been looking for them ever since.

THE END